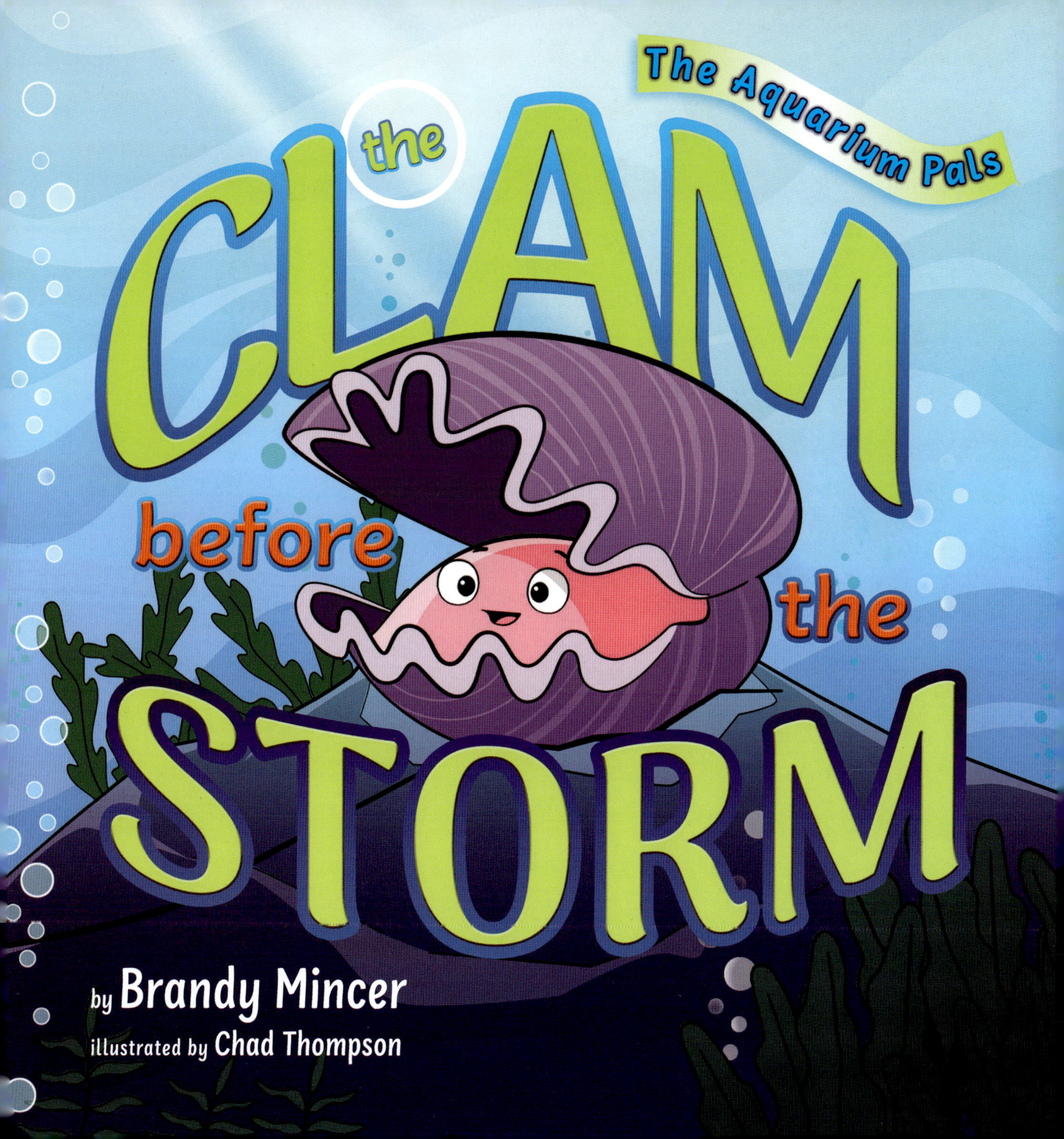
The Aquarium Pals
the CLAM before the STORM
by Brandy Mincer
illustrated by Chad Thompson

First printing: March 2026

New Leaf Press, P.O. Box 726, Green Forest, AR 72638

New Leaf Press is a division of the New Leaf Publishing Group, LLC.

ISBN: 978-0-89221-779-3
ISBN: 979-8-90092-011-5 (digital)

Library of Congress Control Number: pending

Managing Editor Pam Gibbs
Illustrated by Chad Thompson

Printed in China

Visit our website for other great titles:
www.masterbooks.com

For information regarding promotional opportunities, contact the publicity department at pr@nlpg.com.

New Leaf Press
A Division of New Leaf Publishing Group
www.newleafpress.com

To my husband, Tony, thanks for pushing me to dream bigger. To my sons, Joshua and Elijah, for always making me laugh. And to my mom, Loretta, who has remained calm through the storm.

Where the beautiful colors of the coral sparkle, a group of little sea creatures live. They aren't just any sea animals; they are a special group of friends who dive deep in their faith to help each other when troubles arise.

First, is Fay Ray. She has beautiful white spots on her back that shine like stars when she swims in circles.

Sid Squid is
a colorful
friend that
can hide
in a flash!

Olivia Octopus has small tentacles,
but that doesn't stop her from helping others.

Next is Gail Whale. She loves to sing songs and gives the best advice.

Stella Starfish takes a while to get places but is usually the first one to arrive at the truth.

Peter Pufferfish can get upset easily, but he has a big heart.

The happiest member of the pals is Sam Clam.
He loves to sit and watch the bubbles float up from the sand.

One day while he was looking up from his spot on the rock,
he felt a sudden WHHOOOOOSH behind him.

He didn't see what caused the water to move, and that scared him. His mind started turning and turning. Then he had a frightening thought... maybe a STORM was coming!

Sam Clam said to himself, *I have to warn my friends about this storm* ***so they can hide!***

First, he saw Sid Squid and Stella Starfish. "A STORM is coming, a STORM is coming!" yelled Sam Clam. "We have to hide!"

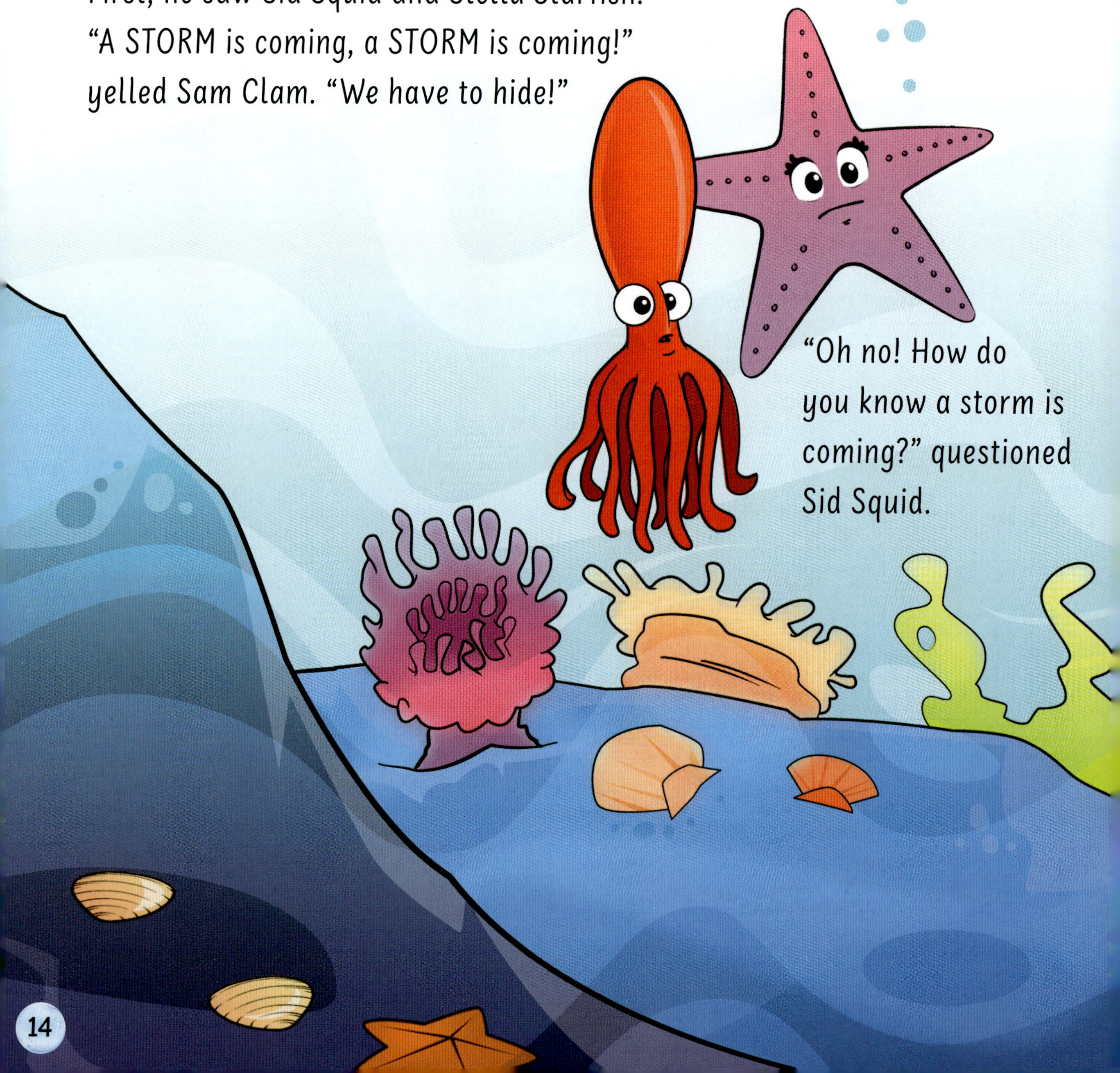

"Oh no! How do you know a storm is coming?" questioned Sid Squid.

"I felt a WHHOOOSH!" cried Sam Clam.
"That has to mean that a storm is on its way."

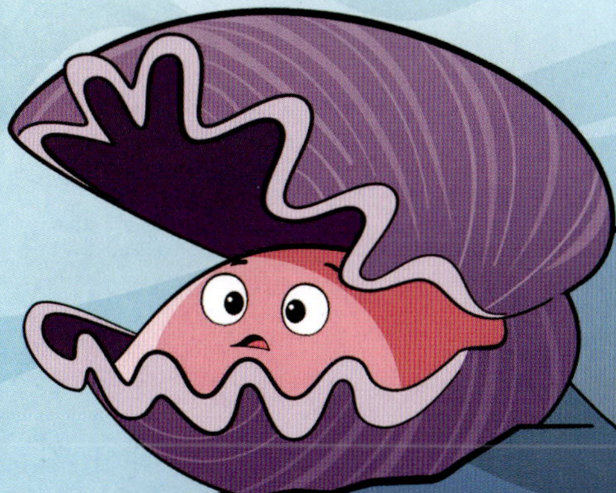

"You're right, Sam.
We have to tell everyone!"

While the three friends were talking,
Fay Ray and Gail Whale swam over.

"What's wrong, guys?"
asked Gail Whale.

Sam perched himself on top of a rock.

"A STORM is coming, a STORM is coming!" yelled Sam Clam.

"We have to hide!"

Fay Ray's eyes got bigger. "That does not sound good, but how do you know a storm is coming?" questioned Fay Ray.

"He felt a WHHOOOSH!" cried Sid Squid. "Surely that means a storm is coming."

While the five of them were getting more scared, Olivia Octopus swam over.

"Why is everyone acting so crazy?"

"A STORM is coming, a STORM is coming!" yelled Sam Clam. "We have to hide!"

"A storm! Oh my goodness.
I've never even seen a storm before.
But, how do you know one is coming?"
questioned Olivia Octopus.

"It was the WHHOOOSH that he felt!"
explained Sid Squid and Fay Ray.
"That means that a storm is on its way."

All the young friends were becoming upset about the coming storm when Myrtle Sea Turtle slowly floated by. "Why are you all so scared?" Myrtle asked.

"Sam Clam felt a WHHOOOSH!"
they all said with shaky voices.
"And now a STORM is coming!"
Myrtle Sea Turtle quietly looked
at all the little friends' faces.

“I’ve been alive for over 100 years,” explained Myrtle Sea Turtle. “You all are so young that you didn’t know we live in an AQUARIUM! A storm could never happen here.”

Just then, Sam Clam felt the WHHOOOSH again. **“There it is! It’s the WHHOOOSH!”** he shouted. They all turned and looked to see...

...the scuba man cleaning the glass.

Myrtle Sea Turtle spoke as they were all watching the scuba man. “Before I lived here, I lived in the ocean. I’ve seen many storms in my life. Storms happen, but storms also go away. They don’t stay forever.”

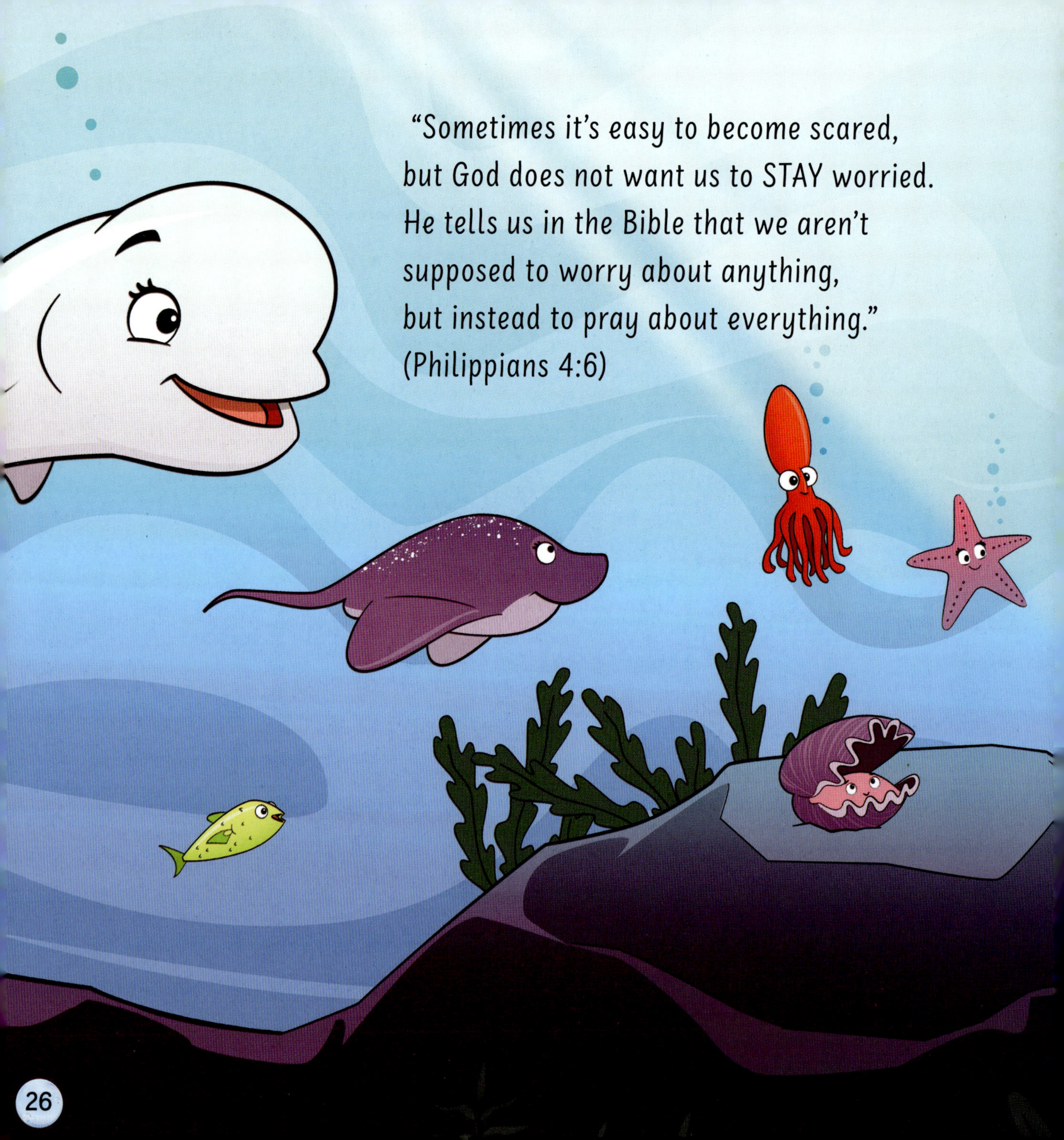

"Sometimes it's easy to become scared, but God does not want us to STAY worried. He tells us in the Bible that we aren't supposed to worry about anything, but instead to pray about everything." (Philippians 4:6)

"So, the next time I feel upset, I should remember to pray to God about my fears instead of staying afraid?" asked Sam Clam.

"Yes!" answered Myrtle Sea Turtle "He will hear you and help to calm you. He has everything under control, even when we can't see it."

There are times when we can become scared. We might feel this way when going to a new school or having a new baby brother or sister. Even in the dark, God is still in control and knows our fears. He doesn't want us to continue to be scared. He wants us to talk to Him and ask for help. Remember these verses: "Don't worry about anything; instead, pray about everything. Tell God what you need and thank Him for all He has done. Then you will experience God's peace, which exceeds anything we can understand"
(Philippians 4:6–7; NLT).

More great books from this author:

Fay Ray Finds Her Way

Sid Squib Fibs

Stella Starfish Saves Christmas

Gail Whale Almost Fails

Peter Pufferfish and the Perfect Present

Olivia Octopus and Her Little Limbs